FIRST STORY

First Story aims to celebrate and foster creativity, literacy and talent in young people. We're cheerleaders for books, stories, reading and writing. We've seen how creative writing can build students' self-esteem and self-confidence.

We place acclaimed authors as writers-in-residence in state schools across the country. Each author leads weekly after-school workshops for up to twenty-one students. We publish the students' work in anthologies and arrange public readings and book launches at which the students can read aloud to friends, families and teachers.

For more information and details of how to support First Story, see www.firststory.org.uk or contact us at info@firststory.org.uk.

Deafening Whispers
ISBN 978-0-85748-122-1

Published by First Story Limited
www.firststory.org.uk
Sixth Floor
2 Seething Lane
London
EC3N 4AT

Typesetter: Avon DataSet Ltd
Designer: Ian Norris
Printed in the UK by Intype Libra Ltd

First Story is a registered charity number 1122939 and a private company limited by guarantee incorporated in England with number 06487410. First Story is a business name of First Story Limited.

Deafening Whispers

An Anthology

BY THE FIRST STORY GROUP
AT BABINGTON COMMUNITY COLLEGE

EDITED AND INTRODUCED BY ANDY CRAVEN-GRIFFITHS | 2014

As Patron of First Story I am delighted that it continues to foster and inspire the creativity and talent of young people in challenging secondary schools.

I firmly believe that nurturing a passion for reading and writing is vital to the health of our country. I am therefore greatly encouraged to know that young people in this school – and across the country – have been meeting each week throughout the year in order to write together.

I send my warmest congratulations to everybody who is published in this anthology.

Camilla

HRH The Duchess of Cornwall

Contents

Miscellaneous

Thank You

Kate Kunac-Tabinor and all the designers at OUP for their overwhelming support for First Story.

Ian Norris for giving his time to design the cover for this anthology.

Melanie Curtis at **Avon DataSet** for her overwhelming support for First Story and for giving her time in typesetting this anthology.

Helen Davies for her meticulous copy-editing and her enthusiastic support for the project.

Intype Libra for printing this anthology at a discounted rate and **Tony Chapman** of Intype for his advice.

Arts Council England, the Dulverton Trust and the HDH Wills 1965 Charitable Trust (The Martin Wills Fund) who supported First Story in this school.

HRH The Duchess of Cornwall, Patron of First Story.

Thanks to:
Arts Council England, Authors' Licensing and Collecting Society, Jane and Peter Aitken, Ed Baden-Powell, Laura Barber, BIG Lottery Fund, Suzanne Brais and Stefan Green, the Boutell Bequest, Anthony Clake, Clifford Chance Foundation, Beth and Michele Colocci, the Danego Charitable Trust, Peter and Genevieve Davies, the D'Oyly Carte Charitable Trust, the Dulverton Trust, Dragon School Oxford, the Drue Heinz Trust, the Siobhan Dowd Trust, Edwin Fox Foundation, the Ernest Cook Trust, Esmée Fairbairn Foundation, the Thomas Farr Charity, Martin Fiennes, the First Story Events Committee, the First Story First Editions Club, the Hugh Fraser Foundation, Alex Fry, Garfield Weston Foundation, the Girdlers' Company Charitable Trust, Give a Book, the Golden Bottle Trust, Goldman Sachs Gives, the Howberry Charitable Trust, John Lyon's Charity, Mark Haddon, Kate Harris, Laura Kinsella Foundation, Kate Kunac-Tabinor, Mercers' Company Charitable Foundation, Michael Morpurgo, Millichope Foundation, Nottingham Trent University, Old Possum's Practical Trust, John O'Farrell, Oxford University Press, Philip Pullman, the Pitt Rivers Museum, Psycle Interactive, Laurel and John Rafter, the Sigrid Rausing Trust, Clare Reihill, the Robert Gavron Charitable Trust, the Royal Society of Literature, SAGE, Chris Smith, St James's Place Foundation, the Staples Trust, Teach First, Betsy Tobin, the Trusthouse Charitable Foundation, University College Oxford, Caroline and William Waldegrave, Walker Books, Whitaker Charitable Trust, the HDH Wills 1965 Charitable Trust and the H Steven & P E Wood Charitable Trust.

Most importantly we would like to thank the students, teachers and writers who have worked so hard to make First Story a success this year, as well as the many individuals and organisations (including those who we may have omitted to name) who have given their generous time, support and advice.

Introduction

Andy Craven-Griffiths

In a short time working with these budding young writers I've seen great progress. They've shown continued extra-curricular effort with plenty of moments of inspiration. There have been too many highlights to talk about here but I'd like to mention three particularly pleasing aspects of their journey.

Humour: It is easy to think that writing has to be a serious business, but a streak of humour and a sense of play runs through this anthology, not least in the six-word stories such as Georgie's, 'I gut ful marcs in speling.'

Inventiveness: Everyone has avoided cliché, with brilliant inventiveness in evidence in pieces such as Simon's coded poems, and in the twists at the end of Anthony's *The Robbery* and Daniella's *Assassin!*.

Bravery: All of the pupils' willingness to try something new in writing has been great. Reading that writing out, with a focus on the right tone, intonation, speed, volume, accent and making eye contact, is even more daunting. I have to mention Hibo as the most improved public reader. In March she was barely able to read out in front of the rest of the group. On 1st April, at the University of Nottingham creative writing day, she threw herself into her reading and was unrecognisably, utterly accomplished. As I told her afterwards, she smashed it. I hope all of these young writers will be encouraged to keep taking those risks and trying things out, now they've seen how much they can grow when they do.

A huge thank you finally to Janine and Mark at Babington for their unfaltering commitment to the project.

Foreword

Miss Janine Scott and Mr Mark Penfold

TEACHERS, BABINGTON COMMUNITY TECHNOLOGY COLLEGE

Having no voice is not the same as having nothing to say. Often young people struggle to find appropriate forums for their most creative and private thoughts and ideas. The purpose of this incredible project was to give some of Babington's brightest young minds (in Years 9 and 10) free rein to develop their creative confidence and writing flair.

We are phenomenally proud of the results, which are the culmination of more than four solid months of extra-curricular commitment and hard work. We are even more proud of our students; it has been wonderful watching them discover their own excellence.

In addition, we would all like to thank our writers-in-residence, John Berkovitch and Andy Craven-Griffiths, for their inspirational guidance. We would also like to thank all at First Story for their unrelenting support.

I Come From

I Come From

Iman Egal

I come from not ever knowing where I belong,
from a place where Americans consider us patronising.
A place where war has torn the country apart for more than twenty years,
where I wasn't accepted until my mother fought for us for eight years.
I come from a humongous family and constant visits. A closely knit unit.
I come from the odd, kind person who offers me a beautiful smile.
From long nights, working to get a brighter future,
from short days, where events happen and they fly by in an instant.
I come from racial indifference; passive fascism,
little kids asking why I am forced to wear a dishcloth on my head.
I come from awkward moments.
I come from upside-down semi-detached houses that don't feel like home.
The rare hilarious moments, bringing uncontrollable laughter,
creasing the corners of my eyes.
I come from *SpongeBob*, from *The Fresh Prince of Bel Air,*
repetitive rice and bananas and delicious pasta and sauce.
I come from rich heritage, from individual, colourful characters,

vibrant, colourful dresses and fragrant perfumes.
I come from happiness,
from hardships.
I come from struggle.

I Come From

Megan Sharpe

I come from arguments and breakups, from bruises and fights.
I come from coming and going, from clubland and '80s music.
I come from cheese and literature,
Bangers and mash.
I come from skipping and laughing,
From soaps and horrors, tattoos and piercings,
From a shared bedroom with five children,
From death and tears.
I come from swings and slides,
From Game Boy and Mario.
I come from kissing on the cheeks when you greet.
I come from a posh school.
I come from dad to stepdad, from crying at *Monsters, Inc.*
I come from Gloucestershire.

I Come From

Daniella Southin

I come from *Teletubbies* and *X Factor*
My mum's burnt potatoes
And my sister's legendary fish fingers, chips and beans sandwiches.
I come from a baby doll who lost her leg.
Long spontaneous road trips
And bedtime stories about fairies and Jack Frost.
I come from egg hunting at Easter
Christmas stockings and succulent turkey at Christmas.
I come from the sound of someone screaming, 'Dinner's ready!'
    up the stairs
And the fire alarm going off when my mum burns a cake.
I come from red bricks and cement, rain on sports day.
Dead fish and a scruffy dog.
I come from days filled in another world and Sunday roasts.
Life-long friends who I don't remember not having.
I come from two-day *Harry Potter* marathons
And a love of blue school chairs.
I come from a family who love rock music
And being the youngest of six children.
I come from hand notes
And painted nails.
I come from Leicester.

I Come From

Maryam Mohamed

I come from watching *Power Rangers* every weekend with
my brothers,
From noisy neighbours who rave all night,
From a brother being behind bars not once, but twice.
From a street filled with troublesome teens.
I come from watching the *Tweenies* and hating the bossy one.
From pushing my little brother down the stairs,
From receiving my first pair of trainers at five, it was cool.
From my dad walking me to school, picking cherries for me
to eat.
I come from, 'Ew, what's wrong with your chin?'
From Upendi and Simba and watching *The Lion King*.
I come from people taking the steering wheel from my dad's car.
From hundreds of family members I don't even know,
From wearing big, long, patterned dresses that look like
sewn sheets.
I come from teachers always mispronouncing my name,
From watching *Goosebumps* and being frightened to death.
I come from that game about the theme park and Mario 64.

I Come From

Sarah Adams

I come from the smell of shepherd's pie with creamy mash
and peas,
An Irish dad and a mum from Beaumont Leys.
I come from fights with a little brother addicted to *Ben 10*,
Music from the 80s, 90s and Capital FM.
I come from swingball, netball and uniforms,
From fall-outs at school, exams and name-calling.
'Smarty pants', 'teacher's pet', and 'smart arse'.
I come from high expectations and dreams,
From only owning jackets and denim jeans.
I come from Leicester City football blaring through the TV.
I come from worn-out trainers and really short hair.
I come from growls, Pedigree Chum and a Staffy called Rex,
Birthday presents, Easter eggs and a tree in the corner.
I come from red bricks, cement and the number nineteen.
Living at the bottom of a hill, protecting my bag and pockets.
I come from Beaumont Leys, Leicester, and fish and chips.
I come from Mario Kart and a Nintendo Wii.
I come from laptops, phones and DVDs.
I come from that scent of shepherd's pie with creamy mash
and peas.

I Come From

Josh Fisher

I come from Leicester,
a house in Beaumont Leys,
another house on Blisset Road.
I come from pizza almost every night,
watching *Adventure Time* on TV,
smelling dog poo in the morning and *Thomas the Tank Engine*.
I come from New College to Babington,
Game Boy to DS,
dad to stepdad.
I come from throwing stones and trick-or-treating,
Pokémon and Zelda.
From a mummy and daddy,
two brothers and a sister.
I come from crying over *All Dogs Go to Heaven,*
laughing over cartoons,
and whining over not getting what I want.
I come from broken legs,
new cousins and baby nephews.
I come from broken hearts and *Star Wars*.
Harry Potter and *The Lion King,*
Most of all
I come from
me.

I Come From

Callum Holland

I come from cul-de-sacs and Teletubby Hill.
I come from bricks and cement, builders and scrap.
I come from motorbikes and cars, engines and tyres.
I come from chips and spaghetti, sweet tea and not coffee.
I come from arguments and shouting,
Heartbeats and marriage.
I come from fighting with brothers, to arguments with sisters.

I Come From

Filsan-Yassin Abdullahi

I come from home-made lasagne and salad,
Not being able to eat anything without cucumbers
And having takeaway once a week.
I come from having four brothers and five sisters,
Extraordinary parents that love me dearly
And an amazing grandmother that cared for me.
I come from Holland.
Moved to England at the age of two,
From leaving my older brothers behind.
I come from getting to pray to Allah (swt),
Communication with him whilst on earth
And doing everything for the sake of Allah (swt).
I come from having to go to mosque four times a week,
My father nagging me to finish the Qur'an,
My mosque teacher's excellent voice whilst reading it.
I come from a love for rap music,
Not being able to stop listening to it
Even though it is haram (forbidden) in Islam.
And once in a while listening to nasheeds (Islamic songs).
I come from constantly watching Korean dramas,
The love for action and thriller movies
And my favourite American TV show, *Revenge*.
I come from a love for maths and science,

Aspiring to get A*s for my GCSEs
And having strong intentions of going to university.
I come from worrying about future exams,
Having to do homework for every subject
And the end-of-topic assessments.

I Come From

Hibo Deria

If you believe the media,
I come from:
Civil war: soldiers marching, day in, day out.
Piracy
Brutal murder
Kidnapping
Poverty: skinny from hunger.
Screaming pain
Illegal alien migration
Heartache
Discrimination: the wrong colour, the wrong heritage.
Racism
Prejudice
Criticism
Stereotypes: terrorists taking over.
Disrespect
Embarrassment
Disbelief: no sense of support.
Accusation
Cynicism
Violation
Weakness: fragile hearts.

In reality,
I come from:
Community: working together, caring together, standing by each other.
Wealth
Delight
Pleasure
Impartiality
Equality
True respect
Strength: mental and physical.
Steadfastness
Determination
Pure talent: intoxicating football skills.
Sentimentality
Tradition: constant intake of rice and pasta.
Heritage
Enthusiasm
Sophistication
Endurance: empowered by difficulty.

I Come From

Safia Hassan

I come from continuously eating rice and pasta with a side dish of salad and sweetcorn.
I come from Fariho Frisco's music blasting along with cheers and Nikki (booty shaking).
I come from practising religion and encouraging peace.
I come from inventive hand art and painting soles with neon orange.
I come from *EastEnders*, from a loving mother.
I come from trying to get the latest style and receiving last year's.

I Come From

Georgie Lee

I come from *Clifford the Big Red Dog,*
from the smell of a fry-up, Nike shoes and GTA.
From the sound of the waves on Skegness beach.
I come from my PS3.
From red bricks and cement, the taste of carnival doughnuts,
from friendship and
the barking and meowing of my cat and dog.
I come from Leicester.
From the nagging of teachers,
I come from Skittles, Cadbury's Caramel and crinkly crisps,
from the greeting of hugs,
the respect of my family,
amazing tasting Pot Noodles (the chicken one).
I come from the Milkybar Kid advert.

I Come From

Simon Robinson

I come from mountains and lakes,
Grey, darkness and silence.
I come from fighting with siblings
And from cars and benches.
I come from glasses and bad internet.
I come from binary and Morse.
I come from charging at walls.
I come from insanity
And hallucinations.
I come from games
And insomnia, fearing the darkness.
I also come from elevators, cars and claustrophobia.

.. / -.-. --- -- . / ..-. .-. --- --

Simon Robinson

.. / -.-. --- -- . / ..-. .-. --- -- / -- --- ..- -. - .- .. -. ... / .- -. -.. / .-.. .- -.- . ...

--. .-. . -.-- --..-- / -.. .- .-. -.- -. . ... / .- -. -.. / ... .. .-.. . -. -.-. .

.. / -.-. --- -- . / ..-. .-. --- -- / ..-. .. --. .... - .. -. --. / .-- .. - .... / ... .. -... .-.. .. -. --. ...

.- -. -.. / ..-. .-. --- -- / -.-. .- .-. ... / .- -. -.. / -... . -. -.-. ....

.. / -.-. --- -- . / ..-. .-. --- -- / --. .-.. .- ... ...

.- -. -.. / -... .- -.. / .. -. - . .-. -. . -

.. / -.-. --- -- . / ..-. .-. --- -- / -.-. .... .- .-. --. .. -. --. / .- - / .-- .- .-.. .-.. ...

.. / -.-. --- -- . / ..-. .-. --- -- / .. -. ... .- -. .. - -.--

.- -. -.. / .... .- .-.. .-.. ..- -.-. .. -. .- - .. --- -. ...

.. / -.-. --- -- . / ..-. .-. --- -- / --. .- -- . ... --..--

.- -. -.. / .. -. ... --- -- -. .. .- --..-- / ..-. . .- .-. .. -. --. / - .... . / -.. .- .-. -.- -. . ...

.. / .- .-.. ... --- / -.-. --- -- . / ..-. .-. --- -- / . .-.. . ... - .- - --- .-. ... --..-- / -.-. .- .-. ... / .- -. -.. / -.-. .-.. .- ..- ... - .-. --- .--. .... --- -... .. .- .-.-.-

Haiku

I think of nothing
My mind is always a blank,
Blank, blan , bla , bl , b
Callum Holland

Two rings, two people
A change in their future lives
Eternally bound.
Josh Fisher

Pikachu evolves
Use a Thunderstone on it,
Out comes Raichu, *&^%!
Josh Fisher

Once I was a kid
Then they took my unicorn
Life wasn't the same.
Iman Egal

Boys play with girls' minds
Like women are all a game.
All toys get broken.
Megan Sharpe

Maryland is sick
The chicken is very nice
Finger lickin' good
Iman Egal

The sun shines brightly
The coloured leaves start to fall
Snow tumbles slowly.
Sarah Adams

I'm going bowling
I started when I was four
I used the green shed.
Anthony Grant

To you, it's a bench:
Somewhere to sit in the park.
To me, it's a bed.
Muna Farah

Six-Word Stories

Poo on carpet. Dog was out.
Georgie Lee

In shop. Crisps, chocolate... I'm out!
Georgie Lee

I gut ful marcs in speling.
Georgie Lee

Love note, crumpled in my pocket.
Georgie Lee

The perfect murder; the perfect villain.
Georgie Lee

Pen, paper, words, scribbles, overworked writing.
Maryam Mohamed

Wanted it, got it, lost it.
Amy Blackmore

Candle left unattended; Kerry's ashes remain.
Amy Blackmore

High school: battles, betrayal and blood.
Maryam Mohamed

Goalkeeper dives. Fifty thousand broken hearts.
Simon Robinson

Shampoo-conditioner, towel, straighteners, dryer, vanity appeased.
Simon Robinson

Starting line. Breathless. Hurting. Finish line.
Simon Robinson

Accident, denial, anger, bargaining, depression, acceptance.
Simon Robinson

011 001 100 001 100 110.
Simon Robinson

'I'll do it tomorrow,' said Romeo.
Muna Farah

Flour, sugar, eggs, heat, joy, guilt.
Simon Robinson

One Hundred Word Stories

The Robbery

Anthony Grant

The plan is simple. Bank robbery.

We get there early to catch them off guard. Everything runs smoothly. Soon enough we're loading the money into the van and we start to drive.

Back at the hideout, officers are waiting.

The chase is on.

I'm ready for this. I put my foot down. The sirens are blazing behind me.

They go left, I go right.

These are my streets.

The shortcut pays off; I was trained for this.

BANG! The side of the road; the last of them caught.

'Good work Sarge,' says one of my men.

'We got them.'

My Witch Trial

Sarah Adams

The flames wash over my feet. Is this how I die? Burned at the stake for something I didn't do?

Witch trials have turned this town crazy. Neighbour has turned on neighbour; friends have turned against friends. All I did was light a black candle, a witch's source of power. As my mistress entered my room, she saw the candle. She dragged me to the police. 'GUILTY' was the only word I heard at my trial.

The flames burn my skin. Looking down, my legs are black... just like my candle. That is the last thing I ever see.

Judgement Day

Safia Hassan

I stand there, confused, sweat dripping down my face as the sun is drawn closer. Millions of people surround me. Mankind and Jinn-kind alike all focused on this thing. It towers over us; its shadow blocks out the sun. A thousand shivers run down my spine, neck hairs standing to attention like soldiers ready to march. Everyone departs: scared, worried and confused about where to go.

Then… I see the sign of Kafir. Relief overwhelms me. I am protected now. I know a safe place awaits me. Happily, I have done well, and I hope people have the same mercy.

Confession

Filsan-Yassin Abdullahi

'Obsessed by their stately home (aquamarine pool, Bentley with real leather seats), I couldn't stop my visits. I had never witnessed such lavishness. I stalked, unnoticed… until that day. I snuck into the house and saw their first edition of *To Kill a Mockingbird*. The woman was a relative of my father. I was on the verge of introducing myself when she screamed; the knife was right there… I was getting ready to leave and the little girl woke up. She wouldn't stop screaming,' he cried. 'She just wouldn't stop screaming.'

Chip Shop

Muna Farah

A busy day at the fair, lights illuminating everything in sight as the once bright blue sky began to darken. My stomach rumbled and mumbled like a volcano about to erupt.

The marvellous fragrance of fresh fish and chips tilted my head in their direction. Before I knew it, the scent had pulled me in front of the counter. It was as if my eyes were a metal detector, searching for those strips of golden treasure.

I did it again: burnt the roof of my mouth with my impatience. Every other chip would trigger the tip of my mouth.

The Dark Side

Daniella Southin

I run. It is chasing me… taking me… killing me. I can't escape. It is there; it is always there. I can smell the blood oozing from my wounds, trickling off my fingertip.

A slither of hope fills my heart as I sight a clearing ahead, swamped with light. Cold bitterness engulfs me each time I catch a glimpse of light, swarms me like bees before I get there. I stop… accepting my fate. I fall to the floor, tears streaming down my cheeks. I close my eyes, sensing my soul being torn away. Death…

Meaningless

Maryam Mohamed

Cold, hard steel penetrates skin, slicing into my heart. The blade cuts through the maze that is my body as far as it can go. Blood leaks from my wound, warm and thick. Unbearable pain. It is certain that this is where I shall die. My life is now rapidly coming to an unexpected halt... No time to bid my loved ones farewell. No time to accomplish all of those dreams I said I would eventually make reality. Eventually. When would eventually have been? Never, that's when. Countless days... no, years, wasted. Meaningless. Meaning less.

Recipes

Recipe for a Perfect Mind

Simon Robinson

Take one empty vessel
Drown it in imagination
Spread in some knowledge
Heat up with known facts
Sprinkle in some insanity
Mix in with some emptiness
Wait ten years to mature
Add a teaspoon of fantasies
Knead in a dash of fear
Sieve in some creativity
Bake in memories.

Recipe for the Perfect Camping Trip

Daniella Southin

Ingredients:

1 starry night, like glitter on a child's picture.

A handful of rustling leaves, scorched and crusty from months of heat.

1 crackling, blistering campfire, slicing through the darkness like a knife.

1 rusty truck with memories of children napping in the back seat and countless trips to Tesco.

1 wild deer with a loathing for intruders.

1 rope and a lake to swing over.

A weekend of luminous, sunny weather.

4 crazy friends.

Method:

Start with the starry night.

Sprinkle a handful of flimsy tents and a handful of rustling leaves.

Pour in the crazy friends and let conversation boil over the romantic fire.

Leave to simmer over a weekend of sunny weather.

Stir in the rope and lake for hours of laughter.

Throw in the wild deer and leave to bubble up some frightening excitement.

Blend in the rusty truck, leaving out the fuel.

Take one hilarious walk home.

Sleep!

Recipe for a Perfect Book

Callum Holland

Handful of imagination
Unspecified amount of unpredictability
A dash of action
Sprinkle of backstory
A pinch of betrayal
250 pages of hunger.

Recipe for a Best Friend

Sarah Adams

Take a faithful person,
Add a tablespoon of trust and a sprinkle of loyalty.
Then mix in a generous amount of kindness.
Dash in a hint of jealousy and anger.
Drop in things-in-common and stir thoroughly.
Take a pinch of tissues dried with tears and add to the mix.
Then add a teaspoon of gossip and sleepovers.
Stir until the mixture is smooth.
Add flavourings of advice and issues,
Mix in hugs and soothing words.
Stir in a teaspoon of mood swings and mixed emotions.
Take a cup of music and parties and slowly add to the mix.
Add a pinch of arguments and fall-outs,
And a dash of making up.
Throw in a pinch of running mascara moments
And makeover parties.
Stir until the mixture is smooth.
Bake until perfect.
Enjoy your best friend!

Rewind

Winning the Cup

Georgie Lee

We've won!
Ref blows the final whistle…
Coke flies off the floor with every last bit jumping back into its cup.
Loud screaming,
Striker puts the ball down in the goal,
The crowd drops down to its seats.
The ball flies over the keeper and lands on the striker's foot.
He pulls his leg back and swivels his hips.
Running backwards, the goal gets further away from him.
His legs shaking.
Teammates mumbling to pass the ball.
Sweat running up his face, his forehead soaking it up like a sponge.
The crowd chanting, '!dnalregnE, dnalregnE, dnalregnE'
Fifteen seconds left on the clock to score.

Binary Palindrome

Simon Robinson

0110011001100110011001100110011001
1001100110011001100110011001100110
0110011001100110011001100110011001
1001100110011001100110011001100110

0110011001100110011001100110011001
1001100110011001100110011001100110
0110011001100110011001100110011001
1001100110011001100110011001100110

0110011001100110011001100110011001
1001100110011001100110011001100110
0110011001100110011001100110011001
1001100110011001100110011001100110

The Resurrection

Hibaaq Deria

There I lay. Motionless.

With a trembling breath, I awoke.
I felt as if life had been blown into me,
like a blown-out candle, relit for a second chance.

The spilt blood absorbed back into my body,
my veins like a sponge.

A silhouette running towards me, gripping his blade.

I collapsed upwards, gravity reversed,
and stood face-to-face with the stranger.
It was each man for himself.

The bloody knife struck, and came out wiped clean by my body.
That was a feeling I had remembered.

My hand went to my wound,
I was expecting agony, but found tranquility.
I stood in front of this guy, ready to fight him.
With my eyes closed, I took a deep breath.

But I opened my eyes to
Complete
Emptiness.

Weather

Weather Forecasters

Hibaaq Deria

My friend's face was the sun, blinding.
My heart illuminated like the moon.
Her mind scattering like the clouds.
Her emotions unexpected,
a stalking cloud you can ignore until it rains.
And her life changing like the seasons.
You see, my friend was always switching.
So unpredictable.
Annoying one day, soggy the next,
tropical yesterday, numbing today.
The fact that I could read my friend was ordinary,
I guess friends are the best weather forecasters.

Storms of Heartache

Sarah Adams

The sudden shot of pain hurts like thunder.
The tears roll down like raindrops on windows.
The repetitive snapshots of lightning play the same scene
on repeat.
Him saying, 'It's over.'
No matter how bad it hurts, it goes on, systematically throwing
jabs of pain.
It goes on for what feels like forever.
The sunlight leaks through the clouds.
Trying to break through the darkness but it can't.
Raindrops spot the pavement like tears on a pillow,
They break free even though they are fought back.
After a while of shots of suffering,
The sun breaks through.
It clears the dark clouds and replaces them with a blue sky.
Sunlight shows the way to happiness and getting over the storm.
The heartache eases after the sunlight has wrapped me in its heat.
The dried tears and raindrops leave broken memories in
their wake.
The storm of heartache has vanished… for now.

When I Was Ten

When I Was Ten

Callum Holland

The scent of cats and dogs in the living room.
Mum and Dad talking while the dogs bark.
My sister chatting to me over Game Boy music.
The taste of Mum's spag bol is delicious, Kia-Ora juice.
The old carpet that gave me loads of burns.
Grass and dirt from the garden.
Wet and cold outside, warm inside.
The park behind a block of houses.
Friends playing up the road, little brothers fighting.

When I Was Ten

Sarah Adams

The birthday party that lasted ages,
Purple, pink and white balloons hung on walls.
The mellow tones of 'Happy Birthday' songs.
The high-pitched sound of the shouted, 'SURPRISE!'
The tang of oranges and apple juice.
The silky smoothness of my dark, black dress.
Tight, shiny black shoes made my feet ache loads.
Shiny, coloured jewels on brand new earrings,
Sweet taste of frosting on my birthday cake.
The hush of children playing hide-and-seek.

When I Was Ten

Josh Fisher

Charmander, Bulbasaur, Squirtle to choose,
The hardest part is to let them out loose,
Vomit, breath, sweat, all upon a stage,
Teachers say, 'Turn the page, now, turn the page!'
The seaside, cotton candy and all that,
One time, at my dad's, I saw a huge bat.
Shouting, arguments, it wasn't great,
Tell you what was, watching *Yu-Gi-Oh!*
Hospital beds, blood, cuts and boo-boos.
That was when I was ten, how about you?

When I Was Ten

Megan Sharpe

I smell the smoke of a cigarette tip,
I hear the sound of shouting,
Screaming kids, rocking my bed side-to-side,
I hear dogs and Dad breathing heavily.

The tang and freshness of Coca-Cola,
The succulent taste of chicken.

I feel the pain of lost family,
Disappointment, unloved, insecure, wrong.

I see the welcoming hands of my nana,
I see cars passing by,
I see an insecure little girl who is being bullied.
And that there are two sides to every person.

If Love Was

If Love Was

Filsan-Yassin Abdullahi

If love was a Korean drama, I would be the leading actress.
If love was dancing with the stars, I would be the dancers.

If love was Lil Wayne 'Drop the World' ft. Eminem, I'd be the DJ.
If love was a sculpture, I would be the clay.

If love was a flower, I would be the stem.
If love was expensive, I would be a gem.

If love was maths, I'd be the calculator.
If love was a language, I would be the translator.

If love was a Bentley, I would be the wheels.
I love was shoes, I would be the heels.

If love was a belly, I would be the feeder.
If love was the holy Qur'an, I would be the reader.

If Love Was

Muna Farah

If love was a shoe, I'd be the laces
If love was a picture, I'd be the faces
If love was teeth, I'd be the braces

If love was the sky, I'd be the stars
If love was a prison, I'd be the bars

If love was yin, I'd be yang
If love was a drum, I'd be the BANG

If love was a bed, I'd be the sheets
If love was a table, I'd be the seat

If love was a drug, I'd be the high
If love was the internet, I'd be Wi-Fi

If love was a keyboard, I'd be the mouse
If love was a wife, I'd be the spouse

If love was a bin, I'd be the trash
If love were beans, I'd be the mash

If love was a pen, I'd be the paper
If love was pregnancy, I'd be the labour

If love was the devil, I'd be an angel
If love was a cop, I'd be the bagel

If love was a razor, I would be hairy
If love was my hand, I'd be the Blackberry

If Love Was

Simon Robinson

If love was data
I would be the hard drive to contain it all.
If love was a car
I would be the wheeler-dealer with the best offers.
If love was like confusion
I would be… erm… something?
If love was memory loss
I would be
If love was… like…
VIRUS DETECTED. Firewall breached. Systematic failure. Shut down in progress.

If love was a car
I would be the dealer with the best offers.
If love was data
I would be the hard drive to contain it allllllllllllll.
If love was memory loss
I would be… I would…
What was I saying again?

Miscellaneous

Teddy Bear

Georgie Lee

Washing away your childhood memories, not remembering how much something so little could mean to you. The only thing that you can talk to, no matter how stupid it may sound. The one who is always getting ragged up by Dodger the dog and then chucked on a bedroom floor. The one who is always being trodden on by the parents after an argument. The one taken everywhere on many adventures. The one who gets the most cuddles every day. The one quickly forgotten and then put in a bag in the attic. The one that makes you remember not to do anything that can put your life in danger; the one that keeps you safe. The one who, when you lose them, it feels like you've lost everything.

Secret Message

Sarah Adams

Bunches of people thought Rose was normal
It was apparent that they thought this
Rose was different, her eyes were as red as fire
Different how, you ask? Well

Once the new guy came to town her life changed
Forever!

For Rose's secret would shock the world
If her secret got found out, that is
Rose was something new... Her
Exciting secret is hidden in this poem.

My Storage Nightmare

Georgie Lee

I sit there every day with my family, in a row, in order. I smell brand new but my family smell old. I've only just joined the family. I don't want to leave them, but the time is coming when the humans will come and take me again. Putting their disgusting hands all over me, staring at my blurb. They have already taken my brother. I wasn't even born when it happened, but my parents told me about it all. Those disgraceful humans use us; they exploit us. They take us home, turn us over and then close us. After that, we are either put up on a nice shelf with a new family or put in the attic with the rest of the low life pages. I hate my life, the bend in my spine. Why couldn't I just be a cat or a dog or a bird? They live their lives free, sometimes. I can't live like this; it's not fair. I see a shadowy figure. I must leave!

Assassin!

Daniella Southin

1847

Elizabeth braced herself for the tight pull of her basque. Elizabeth loathed going to balls, despite the fact that she looked stunning in the ball gowns with her tall, slender figure. The handsome men always asked her to dance and she always would. They would try to replicate those perfect moments of a tender kiss on the terrace with the quilt of stars above her, just like every girl dreamed of – except her. Every time a guy tried to impress her, she would just play along to see if once – just once – one of them would do something extraordinary, something different. A different way they traced their perfectly buffed hands along her hard-set jaw line. A different way they looked into her stern, rejecting eyes as they leaned in to kiss her tender lips. She wanted someone she wouldn't have to be fragile for just so they could feel masculine and confident.

Isabelle, Elizabeth's maid, bowed the bottom of her basque and handed her a lacy dress. Behind the dressing screen, Elizabeth slid gently into what she thought was a monstrosity of a gown. She was encaged in material that restricted her natural ability to leap and bound. Elizabeth stared down at herself, appalled by what she saw despite the beauty that was radiating from her.

When she finally reappeared in the centre of the room, Isabelle was waiting there ready to tie her hair up tight like the 196 times before.

Roughly twenty minutes later, Isabelle finally let Elizabeth look in the mirror. She looked gorgeous and she hated it. She looked exactly like all the other girls at the ball – caked in a face that wasn't hers.

'What do you think?' Isabelle asked.

'At least I'll blend in,' she thought to herself. Putting on a brave smile, Elizabeth replied, 'It is... It is great, thank you Isabelle.'

'You don't have to go to every ball that your mother organises, Elizabeth. I can see how much you don't want to,' explained Isabelle.

'But I do. If I don't, my mother will be crushed. She wants me to find a husband as much as I don't want to go.'

'One day you will find someone who will love you for who you are, Elizabeth, despite your mur... your flaws,' Isabelle corrected. 'You will not have to go to these balls to try to impress every man you see. You will not have to try to impress your mother. You will not even have to try to impress him because he will love you for what is on the inside, not the outside. You should stop trying so hard and be yourself.'

Elizabeth knew Isabelle was only trying to make her feel better for not having a husband at the age of thirty-three, which was pretty old for a respectable rich woman like her.

...

Elizabeth stood in front of the grand stairs curving into the ballroom. She closed her eyes, preparing herself for the oncoming events. She knew that tonight would be the same as any other, but there was a pinch of hope in her heart that true love might weave itself into her heart. She pushed those feelings down, opened her eyes and hiked up the stairs, strands of her curly brown hair tumbling across her face.

Elizabeth's stiletto heel broke halfway up the stairs and she stumbled straight onto her face.

'Just my luck,' she thought to herself. Never mind, the heel was probably of better use in her hand anyway.

As she blew a piece of hair out of her face, a rough hand reached in front of her. She glanced up to see the most dazzling face she'd ever seen. Elizabeth took his hand as he helped her up. For a moment she stared into his blazing blue eyes and he stared back into her brown ones. One hand was still gently placed in his and the other was still clutching the stiletto like a blade. She hoped to never let go of either.

'Are you okay Miss...?' he started.

'Uh... uh...' Elizabeth mumbled, still gaping at his glorious face. She composed herself a split second later. 'Key, Elizabeth Key. And yes... thanks to you.'

'Lucas Glare. I am glad to be of assistance. If my assistance could stretch as far as escorting you to the ball, Miss Key, I would be most delighted.'

'Well, lucky for you, it does,' replied Elizabeth, gently placing her bare arm on top of his suited one.

They walked in silence into the vast ballroom. Elizabeth couldn't help wondering if this man had fallen from the sky because she had never stumbled over her words like that in front of anyone.

They spent the night laughing, dancing and having the time of their lives. Elizabeth knew that what they had would never last... not after he found out what she was.

They stood on the balcony just outside the ballroom, thousands of stars sparkling above them in the deep night sky.

'You seem so different from every other guy I have ever met, Lucas,' Elizabeth expressed, gazing out into the distance from the edge of the balcony. 'You don't come from a rich family do you?'

'How did you know?' His eyes wandered to the floor.

'I just… I had a feeling.' Elizabeth could not explain it.

'I will take that as a compliment,' he replied.

'So, who are you?'

'My mother and I were alone after my father died…' admitted Lucas. His eyes glazed over at the thought of his late mother.

'Oh…' responded Elizabeth, wide-eyed. 'Erm… I am sorry.'

'You don't have to say anything, Elizabeth. It happened a long time ago. But if you don't think it's suitable to be with someone like me, I understand.'

'No, not at all. I love who you are. I think you are amazing,' Elizabeth replied, glancing at the stars above.

'I think you are amazing too,' and with that Lucas kissed her. Not a peck on the cheek, but a full-on kiss… one like every other guy had tried.

She shoved him away with all her force. Rage, disappointment and frustration bubbled inside of Elizabeth. How could she have been so stupid to think that he would be any different to any other man? Her fists balled up with emotion as thoughts raced through her mind. Then one – one thought stood out in her mind. She knew exactly how she would get her revenge on Lucas, revenge for being like everyone else, revenge for making her think otherwise, revenge for making her fall in love with him. The anger made her stronger; she could feel it in her bones.

She placed her hands upon Lucas' chest and pushed him towards the edge of the balcony. A bead of sweat dripped across his forehead, his hands were trembling and fear radiated off him like an aura. The dancing fierceness in her eyes would be the last thing Lucas ever saw.

She pushed him. She pushed him right over the balcony. She watched as his body fell to the ground, uncontrollable screams escaping the mouth that had touched hers. His lifeless body lay mangled on the floor, limbs bent at impossible angles, blood seeping into the grass, eyes white.

Now he knew. He knew what she was. She was a killer.

The Plant

Megan Sharpe

Our teacher Mr Grant
Brought in a curious plant.
A curious shrub, so small and squat
It sprouted out from its little pot.

He placed it in the corridor
On the table by the door
Each day it grew and grew
And flourished all winter through.

In cold and damp it seemed to thrive
We all wondered how it had stayed alive.
In the summer when it was drier
The plant grew higher and higher and higher.

The stem was brown like river mud
The leaves were bright and red as blood.
The tendrils sticky like glue
Each day the plant grew and grew.

Soon it touched the ceiling high
The plant was reaching to the sky.
Then one cold and frosty day
Our science teacher was away.

No one knew or could explain
Why he was never seen again.
I must admit I found it weird
When the other teachers disappeared.

Then in the library all alone
I found this old and rusty tome.
There was a picture of the shrub
Growing in the jungle mud.

A venomous plant of fearsome height
Its jaw-like leaves with a poisonous bite
And there it said I'm pleased to say,
That teachers were its favourite prey.

I placed the book back on the shelf
And thought I'd keep this to myself.

Baggage

Josh Fisher

I remember this house. It was the house everyone was afraid of at Halloween and the one no one visited to give greetings at Christmas. There would always be moss growing on the walls next to the rotting, red front door. There would also be a stench, like the whole house had been dunked in sewage water. Tales were told of this house, tales that would scare little children and bring horror to the elderly.

To be completely honest, I don't know what this house's purpose was or why it was built. Life has never really been the same since the house was built. There's always something about it that makes me cringe walking past it. People say that an old woman used to live there and something inside the house killed her, but I don't believe it. I used to think it was just a story, until I found out the truth.

The truth was that my mother was the one killed in the house. I had been told lots of things, but I only believe one of them. It was only at the age of ten when I was told what happened by a close family friend, Jill.

Jill said that it was a normal winter night. Snow covered the driveways, front porches and pavements of every house in Violet Berry Street. Jill said that she had seen a strange man walking down the street wearing a black jumper with matching leggings. The man was carrying a bag which looked particularly heavy.

F-Un fair

Amy Blackmore

As I look through the dusty mirror, my reflection is staring right back at me. The younger me is on the other side. That was before it all went wrong...

I am fourteen years of age, at the carnival with my six friends. The screams of the children are constantly ringing in my ears. I watch myself going towards that ride. I try to stop myself, but it is impossible, the younger me can't hear my fists beating against the other side. All of my memories come flooding back, getting on that ride, its sounds, like an evil promise, the pain, the tears. I listen to my friends laughing at the terrified look on my face. Why do they want me to go on the ride?

The Future Can Help Me

Safia Hassan

I remember that day very clearly. I look back at that day wishing that they did not argue, praying that she would come back, but it did not happen. That one day changed my life forever. I remember crying until my eyes dried then going downstairs pretending everything was okay. But it wasn't. Food didn't taste as good. Like Play-Doh. I didn't laugh at my friends' jokes. Even daylight seems dark to me. I see kids with their mothers and that makes my eyes water.

I can't linger on the past, only the future can help me.

Going to England

Filsan-Yassin Abdullahi

When you were two years old, your stepbrothers decided to take you, your sister and your brother to the park. As soon as you guys arrived there, you and your real brother went on the swings. One of them was pushing you and the other one was pushing your brother. I followed them because I thought that you guys would be in danger. I thought they would harm you so that they could annoy me. They did so much to me.

It became so extreme that your father hit me because I told him that what they were doing to me was wrong. It became so extreme that your father chased me with a knife when I'd just got home from giving birth to you. They were fifteen but they still did actions I would expect from a five-year-old.

But this time, it was different; they were acting like true brothers. I was astonished. They were laughing and playing with you without harming you in any way. Why were they being like this? Were they plotting something? Did they know that I had followed them? Many more questions were flowing through my mind. I couldn't believe my eyes. I watched for another half an hour to make sure that I was seeing correctly.

Considering I was pregnant with your younger sister, I became tired of watching and so I turned to go home. As I stepped into the house, I realised that they had taken three children and I had only seen two. I ran. I ran as fast as I could.

When I got to the park, I started searching for my poor daughter who had been taken away by a demon; I saw them in the distance. He was on a scooter and your sister was on the scooter as well. It was like I was in a nightmare. I couldn't move. If I screamed his name, he would turn around and not look at where he was going, therefore he and your sister would fall. All I could do was pray.

My prayer was not accepted because he and your sister fell anyway. They fell and rolled down a hill. I ran to the end of the hill and your sister was at the bottom, then the scooter and then your stepbrother were on top. I felt like dying at that moment.

I ran to get to your sister. She was bleeding from her ear. Your stepbrother was hurt much worse. With your sister under my arm, I grabbed you and your brother. We ran.

We arrived at home. I rushed through the door. I grabbed a suitcase. I threw some clothes in. 'Get the passports!' I screamed. You searched through your father's desk.

We ran out the house. We got into a taxi.

'Where are we going?' your brother said.

'I don't know,' I replied.

The taxi dropped us off at the airport. I scanned the departure board. First available flight? England.

'England,' I said. 'We're going to England.'

We leaned back in our seats. I looked out the window. I left that life behind.

Get Rid

Maryam Mohamed

Burn. Cut. Shock. Drown. Suffocate. These are examples of extreme physical torture. These things are frowned upon in society and that's good, but why do these processes even exist? What gives another person the right? Why do we give others the right? Who are the 'we' who give the right? Who are the 'we' who let monsters rule over us? Why do we give people we hate such power? See that is the thing I never understood about the movie *Mean Girls*. Why did Regina George have so much power in the school? Why was she so feared? No one liked her, yet she was their queen bee. All she did was make everyone else feel lesser, so why want her approval? This applies to the real world, to rulers and celebrities. Why not just get rid?

Wrinkles

Anthony Grant

The deep curves at the side of her mouth are the pride of her son the construction engineer.

The valleys on her head were dug when her sister went out with Chris the loser.

The cobwebs beneath her eyes are the soft silk of a thousand sunrises seen from her balcony.

The ridges on her nose are the mountains of stress from being a mum.

The cracks under her eyes are the story of too many late nights watching *Jeepers Creepers* and *Saw*.

The empty riverbanks near her eyes were eroded by too many tears when her children left home.